PIRATE PRINCESS

More adventures of the

PIRATE PRINCESS

Portia

Pandora

Coming soon

Petticoat

PIRATE PRINCESS

PANCAKE

JUDY BROWN
SIMON AND SCHUSTER

For Max

SIMON AND SCHUSTER
First published in Great Britain by Simon & Schuster UK Ltd, 2007
A CBS COMPANY

1 3 5 7 9 10 8 6 4 2

Simon & Schuster UK Ltd
Africa House
64-78 Kingsway
London WC2B 6AH

A CIP catalogue record for this book is available from the British Library

ISBN 9781416901921
Typeset by Tracey Paris
Printed and bound in Great Britain by Cox & Wyman Ltd, Reading, Berkshire

Contents

King Percy and Queen Doreen
are pleased to invite you to the wedding
of their dear daughter

Princess Pancake
to
Arctic Prince Ivor

at his Ice Palace in the Arctic circle
(please remember to bring your
thermal underwear)

Chapter One

Portia the Pirate Princess dashed out of the Captain's cabin of her pirate ship, the *Flying Pig*, and burst onto the deck. Squawk, her parrot, followed close behind in a flurry of feathers.

'Ahoy, shipmates!' Portia bellowed. 'We need to prepare a rescue mission. Peppermint, Jim, Pandora, meet me in my cabin! Bosun Betty, make ready the sails! We're heading north!'

Portia had been a Pirate Princess ever since she ran away to sea with her ladies-in-waiting. Her parents had wanted her to marry the ghastly Prince Rupert, so she sold her crown to buy a ship and now lived a life of adventure on the ocean waves. Her mission was to rescue other princesses unhappy with their lot. She had already been joined by her cousin, Princess Peppermint, and an old friend from school, Princess Pandora. Not wanting to miss out on the fun, Pandora's sister Sophie had joined them, too.

Portia had placed an ad in the *Princess Daily News* which gave hope to princesses in peril all over the world, and Squawk had just delivered the latest letter in answer to the ad.

'OK, everyone, gather round!' said Portia, as Peppermint, Pandora and First Mate Jim entered her cabin. The four of them stood round the table, which was covered with maps and charts. 'I've had a letter from Princess Pancake.'

Portia picked up the letter and began to read.

Dear Portia
Mother and Father have chosen a Prince for me and, as I feared, it's Arctic Prince Ivor. He's not a bad sort, I know, but his palace is made entirely of ice. They don't have a normal kitchen because the palace would melt so I'll never be able to cook again. Everything Aunt Delia taught me will be wasted, and I've just perfected my recipe for sticky-toffee pudding.
Please, please, rescue me.

Yours hopefully,
Princess Pancake

PS I'll bring all my recipe books.
PPS Hope you enjoy the package.

'And this,' said Portia, 'is the package that came with the letter.'

She unwrapped the tiny package and took out a shiny chocolate. 'Give me your penknife, Jim.' Jim passed his penknife to Portia, who cut the chocolate into four pieces and handed them out. 'Pancake makes the best chocolates you've ever tasted,' she said, popping a tiny morsel into her mouth. 'Mmmmmm,' she purred. 'Delicious!'

The others copied their Captain and munched thoughtfully. Twiggy, the ship's cat, jumped onto the table to lick up the crumbs.

'Wow! This is incredible!' exclaimed Peppermint, trying not to dribble.

'Fantastic!' agreed Pandora, licking her lips.

'Mmmmmmmmmmmm...' murmured Jim, eyes closed.

'Pancake's cooking is legendary,' Portia went on. 'She's been cooking ever since she could hold a spoon. Her Aunt Delia, who's one of the most famous chefs there's ever been, taught her everything she knows. Pancake used to bake cakes for us when we were at school. She just loves to cook.'

Jim's face had taken on a dreamy look and now he started to jump up and down.

'If we rescue Princess Pancake,' he asked, 'do you think she'll cook for us?'

'I'm sure there's nothing she'd enjoy more,' replied Portia.

'Wouldn't it be wonderful to have tasty food for a change! I know poor Nancy does her best, but she's about as much good as a chocolate teapot in that galley,' said Peppermint. 'You don't think she'd be upset though, do you?'

7

'Hardly,' Jim chuckled. 'Nancy never wanted to be ship's cook in the first place but no one else would do it. And since she was the only one who'd worked in the palace kitchen, she volunteered.'

'Don't get too excited,' cautioned Portia, raising her hand for silence. 'There's something scribbled on the back of the letter.' She turned it over, frowning slightly. 'It's a bit difficult to read. Looks like she wrote this in a hurry.'

Portia read out loud:

OH NO! COUNT NASTY HAS JUST ARRIVED AT THE PALACE. My parents must have asked him. Whatever you do.
DON'T COME HERE!!

We leave for a state visit to the Ice Palace the day after tomorrow. What am I going to do?
HELP ME PLEASE !!!!

Portia thumped the table with her fist.

'It's going to have to be a rescue at sea!' she said, pointing to the chart. 'This is where Pancake's ship is heading. This is where we are now. And this...' Portia drew a cross on the chart. '... is where our paths need to cross. Jim?'

'Yes, Captain!'

'Plot the co-ordinates and get us on course. Pandora?'

'Yes, Captain!'

'How's that new invention of yours coming along?'

'Actually, it's nearly finished.'

'Excellent! We may need to use it. Squawk?'

'Aye, Cap'n!' squawked Squawk.

'I want you to take this letter straight to Princess Pancake. You know where to go.'

'Squawk!' squawked Squawk and flew out of the window.

'OK, everyone!' said Portia, taking a deep breath. 'This is the plan...'

Two days later, the *Flying Pig* was nearing its destination. Emily, the Ship's Lookout, stood in the crow's nest, scanning the horizon. On deck, Portia was going through final preparations with the crew.

'How do you put on this breathing thing, Pandora?' she asked.

Pandora handed her some instructions. 'These show you how it works,' she said, 'and how to wear it.'

Portia examined the instructions carefully and followed them step-by-step.

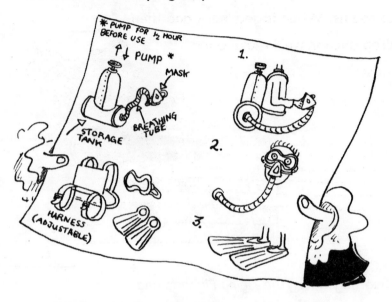

'You're so clever!' said Portia, now wearing the contraption. 'I assume it works. . .'

'Of course it does,' said Pandora, slightly miffed, 'I've tested it myself.'

'Ship ahoy!' roared Emily from the crow's nest. Portia wriggled out of the breathing machine and ran to the bow of the ship. She looked through her telescope.

'That's King Percy's ship all right,' she said with a smile. 'Jim, keep a distance, I don't want them to see us. When it gets dark and they drop anchor, we'll make our move.'

A few hours later, under cover of darkness, the *Flying Pig* drew closer to King Percy's ship. On board, Princess Pancake was busy getting ready for her escape. She'd packed her beloved cookery books in a small chest with a few other things. And she'd put some of her favourite cooking utensils and her collection of herbs and spices in a rucksack. She was just about to go on deck and smuggle them into the

dinghy, when there was a knock on her cabin door.

'Who is it?' asked the Princess warily.

'It's just Nanny Agnes, dear,' replied a creaky old voice outside. 'I thought I could hear noises coming from your cabin. It's very late for you to be up, dear. Can I come in and see if you're all right?'

'No!' said Pancake, a little too quickly. 'I mean, I'm fine, Nanny. Er. . . I fell asleep reading and the book fell off my bed. I'm going right back to sleep now. Good night.'

'All right, dear, if you're sure,' said Nanny Agnes. 'Sleep well.'

Pancake stood by the door and listened until she heard her Nanny's footsteps dying away. She waited a few more moments, picked up her belongings, opened the door gingerly and crept outside. As quietly and carefully as she could, Princess Pancake tiptoed onto the deck and put her precious cargo into the dinghy. Everything seemed really quiet but if she'd looked over her shoulder, she'd have realised that she was not alone.

Back on the *Flying Pig*, Portia, Pandora, Peppermint and Jim prepared for the rescue.

'Are you all clear about what we have to do?' Portia asked. 'Pancake should be waiting for us. I told her to get the dinghy packed and ready to launch. We'll swim over and then row back together.'

'What are these breathing machines for?' asked Jim, looking a little nervous.

'When we get close enough to the ship to be spotted, we're going to swim underwater,' Portia explained. 'We'll swim under the hull to the anchor and climb up the rope. Squawk will fly over and signal to Pancake that we're on our way.'

On hearing this, Squawk flew off in the direction of King Percy's ship.

The rescuers swam across as planned.

The underwater breathing machines worked brilliantly, despite Jim's misgivings, and soon they stood dripping and shivering on the deck of King Percy's ship. Pancake hugged them exuberantly.

'Thank goodness you've come,' she said, as quietly as she could. 'When I saw Squawk fly over the ship, I almost screamed with excitement!'

'It's a good job you didn't,' said Portia, smiling. 'You might have woken the whole ship!'

'I know,' Pancake laughed. 'But everything seems really quiet. I think the night watchman might even be asleep. Maybe it's all the sherry I put in the trifle!'

Suddenly Portia turned round as she heard what sounded like a cackle coming from behind the main mast.

'Who's there?' she whispered hoarsely. 'Show yourself!'

A small, hooded shape moved out from behind the mast.

'Nanny Agnes!' said Pancake, 'Is that you? What are you doing hiding in the shadows?'

'Just looking out for you, dear, like I always do.' Nanny Agnes smiled and a shiver ran down Portia's spine.

'Portia,' said Pancake, 'this is my Nanny, Agnes. Well, she's not *actually* my Nanny. Mummy and Daddy brought her to the palace as my nursemaid when I was a baby, and she's been with me ever since.'

'If you're going to run away, Princess, please take me with you! All I've ever done is look after you. I won't know what to do when you've gone.' Nanny Agnes looked at them all with puppy-dog eyes and a small tear trickled down her cheek.

Pancake suddenly felt terribly guilty.

'Oh, please, can Nanny come with us? I'm sure she won't be any trouble,' she pleaded.

'Well, I don't know,' said Portia frowning. 'What do you think, Jim?'

Jim looked at Nanny Agnes, who smiled at him pathetically.

'I don't suppose she could do much harm,' he said uncertainly. 'You're the Captain, it's up to you.'

Portia looked at Peppermint and Pandora, who shrugged their shoulders.

'OK then, you can come,' she said. 'Anyway, if we leave you here, they may try and force you to tell them where we've gone. But you must keep really quiet. We need to get away before anybody sees us.'

Nanny Agnes rushed over to Portia and kissed her hand gratefully.

'I must just go and get a few things,' she said.

'I'll go with you to make sure you're not seen,' said Portia. She followed Nanny Agnes below decks, as the others got the dinghy ready to lower into the sea. Squawk circled the starry sky above the ship, keeping watch.

'Right, Nanny,' said Portia, 'let's do this as quickly as we can. Which way do we go?'

The old woman pointed to a door at the end of a passage and they crept along in silence.

'Wait out here and keep watch, dear,' she said when they reached her cabin. 'I won't be long.'

Nanny Agnes closed the cabin door behind her and grinned evilly. She trotted over to the corner of the room, picked up a large birdcage and spoke in a whisper to its occupant.

'Well, Balthazar, my pretty, everything's going to plan. That stupid night watchman won't stop us, not after what I put in his cocoa. Count Nasty warned me there would be some sort of rescue attempt and I guessed it would be tonight. We'll collect the reward

money and then we'll be rich! Once we get on their ship, it'll be as easy as pie, you'll see.'

'Easy as pie!' the raven repeated, fixing his beady black eyes on her. 'Easy as pie!'

Nanny Agnes covered the cage with a black cloth, gathered up her bag, which was already packed, and stepped outside the cabin.

'What's that?' asked Portia, pointing to the cage.

'It's my darling pet bird. He's been with me since he was a chick. I couldn't possibly leave him behind. He'd die of a broken heart!'

'Oh, all right,' Portia said impatiently. 'There's no time to argue. Just keep him well away from Squawk or there'll be hell to pay.'

'Of course, my dear,' answered Nanny in a sickly, treacly voice.

They hurried back on deck and bundled Nanny's belongings into the dinghy. Portia and Peppermint helped her into the boat, where she sat beside Princess Pancake, trying her best to look sweet and innocent. Pandora climbed in with the breathing equipment, and Portia and Jim, very slowly and quietly, began to lower the dinghy into the water. The ropes creaked as they stretched through the pulleys, but no one on the ship even stirred, and the dinghy reached the waves with a satisfying slap.

'Your turn, Jim,' whispered Portia.

Jim climbed over the side of the ship and slid down the rope into the dinghy. Portia followed and they cast off and started to row towards the *Flying Pig*.

'Excuse me, Princess Pancake,' said Jim, sheepishly. 'I hope you don't mind me asking and won't think me very rude, but have you brought your recipe books with you?' A blush spread across his cheeks.

'Of course,' she answered. 'I couldn't have left without them.'

Jim's stomach rumbled and he grinned contentedly.

'Strange it was so quiet on your ship,' mused Portia. 'I thought they'd be looking out for us.'

Nanny Agnes pulled her hood down to cover her face. She smiled smugly to herself, and peeped out to watch King Percy's ship grow smaller and smaller, until it disappeared into the night.

Chapter Three

As soon as Portia and the crew were back on board the *Flying Pig*, the ship set sail. As dawn broke, King Percy's ship had been left far behind.

When Pancake emerged sleepily from below decks, she found Portia at the helm, steering the *Flying Pig* well away from the icy north.

'Morning, Pancake!' said Portia cheerfully, 'How did you sleep?'

'Like a log!' Pancake grinned. She filled her lungs with the fresh sea air. 'I just love the smell of the sea!'

'This evening we'll have a welcome feast,' said Portia, handing over the wheel to Jim. 'It's a tradition.'

Pancake's face lit up even more. 'And I shall cook it . . . if Nancy will help me!'

'Delighted!' called Nancy, from below. As Jim had predicted, she was really relieved not to be in charge of the galley any longer.

'Excellent!' said Portia.

Everything seemed to be going brilliantly, but somehow, Portia felt uneasy. There was a nervous, fluttery feeling deep in the pit of her stomach, but she didn't know why.

Meanwhile, below decks, Nanny Agnes was in a tiny cabin with her raven, Balthazar. She took a battered old book from the bottom of her travel bag, dusted off the cover, smiled her most evil smile and rubbed her hands together.

'My favourite book,' she cackled. 'Ye Olde Book of
Potions and Poisons'! Page fifty-three, I think it is... Ah
yes...'

There was a short knock on the door and
Princess Pancake came in.

'Nanny, I came to tell you that— '

Nanny Agnes quickly tried to hide the little book
in her pocket but it fell to the floor. She grabbed it as
fast as she could, but not before Pancake had seen
what it was.

'Nanny! Why on earth have you brought the potion book with you?' Pancake asked suspiciously.

'Oh. . . just for safety, dear,' said Nanny Agnes. 'I wouldn't want it to fall into the wrong hands, would I?'

'I suppose not,' Pancake said hesitantly. 'But maybe I should look after it.'

'No, it's all right, dear. I was just about to lock it away in the medicine chest. Was there something you wanted?' she went on, smiling sweetly.

'Er. . . no. I just came to tell you that I'll be busy preparing a feast all day, so if you need me I'll be in the galley.'

'Oh how lovely, dear! Won't that be nice,' said Nanny Agnes, sucking up to the princess. 'I was just about to have a nap. I didn't sleep too well, you know.'

'OK then, Nanny. I'll send someone to get you when everything's ready.'

Pancake turned and left the cabin.

'Excellent!! That will keep you out of my hair for hours,' cackled Nanny Agnes quietly. 'Now, where was I? Ah yes . . .' She opened the potion book. 'Here we are, Balthazar, Prissy Purple Potion. It says this potion

is guaranteed to turn even the most tomboyish tomboy into the prissiest prig ever born!' She giggled. 'Perfect for that pesky Princess Portia!'

Prissy Purple Potion

Guaranteed to turn even the most tomboyish tomboy
into the prissiest prig ever born.

Ingredients

The juice of two spiders   16 spiders legs
6 flies wings   1 tbsp powdered goats hoof
1 sprig lavender   A pinch of grated nutmeg
1 tsp chopped mandrake root   ½ tsp dried catnip
Cats claws (1 pinch powdered)   1 cup red grape juice

Warning: After 72 hours, the effects of this potion
are irreversible.

1. Remove the spiders' legs and extract the juice.
2. Place the legs in a pestle and mortar, add the flies wings

Nanny Agnes examined the recipe then turned to her
raven.

'Right, Balthazar,' she said, opening his cage,
'while I make the potion, I want you to take this

33

message to Count Nasty. It tells him I'm bringing that pesky princess back with all her silly friends. You can fly out of the cabin window so that no one sees you. I want my   reward ready for me when we return.' She put the note in a little black silk bag, tied it to Balthazar's leg and carried him to the window. 'The dear man is waiting for news back at the palace and, oh, he's going to be so grateful. . . he might even ask me to dinner!'

For a moment a dreamy look came over her face. She stroked Balthazar's jet black feathers and opened the window. 'Off you go then, my pretty, see you soon.'

Nanny Agnes waved her hanky out of the window and blew him a kiss.

No one on deck noticed Balthazar flying away with the message. They were too busy preparing for the welcome feast.

'Swab the deck, Mateys!' said Portia as she organised the crew on the main deck.

'It needs a good scrub!' said Peppermint, getting down on her hands and knees. 'It's been ages since it had a proper clean.'

Most of the activity, however, was going on below deck. Pancake, with the help of Nancy and Sophie, was completely re-organising the galley. She'd found the perfect place for her precious recipe books, arranged her pots of herbs and spices, and put away the cooking utensils she'd brought on board.

'Right then,' she said, when everything was in place, 'what food have we got in the storeroom?'

'Nothing very exciting really,' said Nancy. 'We've got vegetables and chicken, eggs, cheese, dried fish and flour. See for yourself.'

She opened the door to the storeroom and Pancake went inside.

'OK,' said Pancake. 'Get me a pen and paper. Who's best at catching fish on the ship?'

'Probably Bosun Betty,' said Sophie. 'Pandora designed a new fishing rod when we joined the crew, and Betty loves fishing now. Last week she caught an enormous swordfish. It took three of us to haul it on board!'

'Fantastic!' exclaimed Pancake. 'Swordfish steaks are delicious.'

'Not the way I cook them!' Nancy said nervously, seeing the look of horror on Sophie's face.

'Nonsense, tonight they'll be lovely, you'll see,' said Pancake. 'Sophie, can you find Bosun Betty and ask her to start fishing? This is going to be a feast to remember!'

Sophie went up on deck to look for Betty while Pancake and Nancy got out the recipe books and began to make notes and prepare the ingredients for the feast.

For the rest of the day, glorious cooking smells wafted up from the galley. By the time Bosun Betty had hauled in her catch, with the help of Portia, Peppermint and Able Seawoman Anisha, Pandora had

assembled the long planks that they used as the
feasting table, and the ladies-in-waiting had set the
places. They'd even put out plates for Squawk and
Twiggy. By the evening, the sound of the crew's
rumbling stomachs was echoing around the *Flying Pig*.
At last the feast was ready.

'Ahoy, Shipmates!' shouted Portia from the poop
deck. 'Take your places at the feasting table!'

A huge stampede followed as everyone rushed
to be seated.

There was quite a spread.

'This looks incredible,' said Portia, as Pancake
brought up the last few dishes from the galley.
'Thanks, Pancake!'

'My pleasure!' said Pancake proudly, beaming
at Portia. Little did they know that Nanny Agnes had

been doing some cooking of her own.

'She's such a clever girl, my Princess Pancake,' said
Nanny Agnes sweetly, helping herself to a large plate of
tasty-looking food. 'I'm so proud!'

Portia was so busy stuffing her face, all she could

do was nod vigorously in agreement.

Nanny Agnes slyly felt in the pocket of her cloak, where a small bottle of Purple Potion was secreted, and smiled back.

'Any one for fruit punch?' asked Nancy. There were a few doubtful glances amongst the crew. 'It's OK,' she said with a smile, 'it's Pancake's recipe!'

Suddenly everybody wanted to try it. Nancy moved from cup to cup filling them all to the brim, before taking her place at table.

No one noticed as Nanny Agnes held her own cup
under the table and poured in the Purple Potion.
Then Portia stood up to make a toast and, quick as a
flash, Nanny swapped Portia's cup with her own.

'Ahoy, Shipmates!' said Portia, raising a hand for
silence. 'I'm not going to make a boring speech.'
Everyone cheered. 'I just want to welcome Princess
Pancake to the *Flying Pig* and say thank you for the
feast.' She picked up her cup. 'Cheers!' she said, and
drained it in one.

Peppermint stared at Nanny Agnes, who seemed to be watching Portia like a hawk. And, when Portia put her empty cup on the table, Nanny Agnes looked as if she would burst with excitement.

'Jim,' said Peppermint. 'I'm not at all sure about that Nanny Agnes.'

'How do. . . gulp. . . you. . . munch. . . mean?' Jim said, between mouthfuls of food.

'She gives me the creeps somehow.' Peppermint shivered.

'Seems too old to be much trouble,' said Jim, scoffing another chicken drumstick.

'I suppose so,' Peppermint said, unconvinced. The rest of the evening was full of fun and laughter and, by the time everything was cleared away, it was well past midnight. Portia, unusually, was the first to bed.

'Sorry, everyone, I just have to go to bed. I'm really. . . sleepy,' she said with a yawn. 'Thanks again, Pancake.' And she plodded off to her cabin.

'Night, Captain,' said Pancake happily.

Peppermint looked again at Nanny Agnes. There was an expression on her face that she couldn't quite pin down. She looked sort of smug, somehow.

'I'm going to have to keep my eye on you,' Peppermint said to herself as the old woman went off to bed.

Chapter Four

The next morning, no one woke up early.
Eventually, the crew started to emerge, bleary-eyed,
from their cabins and hammocks.

'Has anyone seen Portia?' Pancake asked,
yawning and stretching. 'I want to ask her if there's
anything special she'd like for breakfast.'

'Not me,' said Jim, rubbing his eyes. 'I don't think
she's up yet.'

Peppermint joined them on deck. 'That's not like her,' she said. 'Portia's usually one of the first up. I'm going to check she's OK,' she added nervously.

Jim and Pancake followed as Peppermint went to knock on their Captain's door. There was no answer. Peppermint turned the handle and pushed the door.

'It's locked!!' she said, astonished.

'It can't be. Why would she do that? She never locks the door,' said Jim. 'Maybe it's stuck. Here, let me have a go.' He grabbed the handle and pushed hard at the door with his shoulder. It didn't budge. 'It's locked all right,' he said in a worried voice.

Suddenly a shrill, squeaky voice came from the other side of the door.

'Go away!' it snapped. 'I'm not ready.'

They looked at each other anxiously.

'Captain Portia,' said Jim, unsurely. 'Is that you? You sound a bit. . . er. . . strange.'

'What do you mean?' hissed the voice from inside the cabin. 'And don't call me Captain! My name is Princess Portia. I'll thank you to remember your place when you speak to me!'

Jim stepped back in shock.

'What's wrong with her?' asked Pancake, looking at Jim. 'Is she ill?'

'Of course I'm not ill, you fools! I just haven't finished doing my hair. I'll be out in a minute and, when I am, there are going to be some changes around here!' spat Portia.

Quite a crowd had gathered around Portia's door. They had seen the looks of horror on Pancake, Peppermint and Jim's faces, and now everyone wanted to know what was going on.

Peppermint turned to Pancake.

'This has got something to do with your Nanny Agnes, I'm sure,' she said, and was about to go marching off to find the old woman, when she heard the door being unlocked. It opened abruptly and Portia stepped out.

There was a collective gasp... then total silence. Squawk fell off his perch and Twiggy's fur stood on end. Everybody stared at the Captain of the *Flying Pig*. It was as though she'd been transformed overnight from the bravest Pirate Princess Captain on the seven seas to the prissiest, fluffiest, girly pink princess that ever existed. Portia was wearing the dress she'd worn when she first boarded the ship, but she'd added extra pink bows, frills and ribbons. Her nails were beautifully manicured and her hair was curled into ringlets that bounced on her shoulders like springs. She'd even made herself a cardboard crown!

'What are you all gaping at?' she scowled. 'Haven't you ever seen a princess before?'

'But... you...' began Jim.

'Bow when you speak to me, boy!' snapped Portia. 'And go and brush your hair. You look hideous. And when you've done that, you can plot a course back to the palace, I've a Prince to marry. I'll be in my cabin making wedding plans.' She turned and flounced back into the Captain's cabin.

You could have heard a pin drop.

'She's gone mad!' wailed Donnatella, and started to cry. She wasn't the only one.

'What are we going to do?' Pancake said to Peppermint and Pandora.

'I'm going to get to the bottom of this,' said Peppermint, and disappeared below decks.

A few moments later, she reappeared with
Nanny Agnes in tow.

'Let me go, you nasty girl!' said Nanny Agnes,
trying to wriggle out of Peppermint's grasp.
Balthazar, who'd returned early that morning,
followed her, his big black wings flapping in
Peppermint's face.

'Not until you tell us what you've done to
Portia!' shouted Peppermint.

'I don't know what you're talking about,' Nanny
Agnes said indignantly. 'Let me go at once. Princess
Pancake, help me! This girl has gone crazy.'

'I saw the way she was looking at Portia last
night at the feast,' Peppermint said to Pancake. 'She's
up to something, I'm sure.'

Pancake looked hard at her Nanny, who
blushed ever so slightly.

'Nanny, you haven't! Tell me you haven't!' said
Pancake in horror.

Nanny Agnes said nothing. Pancake turned to
Peppermint.

'Nanny has a special recipe book,' she explained.
'Sometimes she makes potions. But she promised
me—'

'It's got nothing to do with me,' Nanny
interrupted. 'I can't believe you're accusing a harmless
old lady. Boo hoo,' she went on, wailing dramatically.

'Make her walk the plank,' said Jim. '*Then* she'll tell us the truth.' He was angry now and so were the rest of the crew.

'Walk the plank! Walk the plank!' chanted the crew of the *Flying Pig*. Bosun Betty, Anisha and Claire ran across to prepare the plank for Nanny Agnes.

'I think you'd better tell them, Nanny. I don't think they're joking,' warned Pancake.

'Never!' said Nanny Agnes.

They bundled her onto the plank and pushed her half way down.

'There are sharks in the sea, you know!' shouted Pandora.

Nanny Agnes looked slightly less sure of herself and peered nervously at the water slapping six metres below.

'Walk the plank! Walk the plank!' came the chant once more.

Peppermint prodded Nanny with the mop. 'Down to the end with you, or tell us what you did.'

Nanny Agnes wobbled a little further down the plank. Slap, slap, slap, went the waves beneath.

'Oh look! I can see a shark over there,' teased Jim.

'Nonsense!' said Nanny Agnes.

'Oh, yes,' cried Sophie joining in the joke. 'It's a whopper!'

Peppermint pushed Nanny further down.

'Stop it, stop it!' Nanny shrieked. 'Or I'll put a spell on all of you... er... I mean I'll... Oh drat!'

'So it's true!' said Pancake. 'Nanny, how could you?'

'Confess and we'll bring you back on-board,' said Peppermint.

'Oh very well!' Nanny Agnes shrugged. 'It's too late now, anyway.' She drew herself up to her full height (which wasn't very tall) and cackled, 'Yes, it was me! I've turned your precious Captain Portia into a prissy pink princess!'

Chapter Five

Moments later, Nanny Agnes had been un-
ceremoniously dragged back on deck. Pancake
put her hands on her Nanny's shoulders and
looked her straight in the eye.

'If you ever cared for me at all, you'll tell me
exactly what you've done,' she pleaded.

Nanny Agnes felt a tiny twinge of guilt. 'I've given
her a potion, of course,' she said.

'When will it wear off?' asked Peppermint.

'Oh, it won't wear off, my dear,' Nanny Agnes
said with a sickly smile. 'In forty-eight hours it will
become permanent.'

'NO!!' gasped the rest of the crew. Squawk fainted.

'Oh yes!' Nanny Agnes assured them, enjoying their reaction enormously

'There must be an antidote,' said Jim.

Pancake shook Nanny Agnes gently. 'Is there, Nanny? Is there an antidote?'

'Er no, no, there isn't,' Nanny insisted.

'I don't believe her,' Peppermint said. 'Make her walk the plank again!'

'Nanny' said Pancake, 'I want you to look me straight in the eye and swear that you're telling the truth. I know most of your potions have antidotes. Why should this one be any different?'

Despite her evil ways, Nanny Agnes found that she couldn't lie to Princess Pancake. After all, she'd looked after her since she was a baby.

'Oh very well then,' she admitted, 'there *is* an antidote.'

Everyone sighed with relief.

'But you'll never be able to give it to her in time!' Nanny Agnes added smugly.

'Why is that, you evil old woman?' asked Emily.

Nanny Agnes smiled. 'Because the most important ingredient is a rare flower that grows on only one island in the world. It's called the red llima and it grows around a lake beneath a waterfall but you'll never get your hands on it in time.'

'Where is this island?' shouted Jim. 'Tell us now!'

'I don't know where it is,' said Nanny Agnes. 'It's called Garden Island. Nobody lives there and that's all I can tell you.' She folded her arms crossly and refused to say any more.

'But why, Nanny?' asked Pancake, almost in tears. 'Why did you betray me?'

'Count Nasty offered me a huge reward to bring you and the other princesses back. I'll be able to retire and live in the luxury you've always known. Maybe I'll live on Garden Island,' she added with a snigger.

'Count Nasty,' sighed Pandora. 'We should have known he'd be at the bottom of this.'

'Take her below and lock her up,' bellowed Peppermint. 'We've work to do.'

Pancake marched Nanny Agnes, with Balthazar in tow, below decks to her cabin. She opened the door and pushed them inside.

'OK, Nanny, give me that book and your medicine chest, NOW!'

'Shan't!' said Nanny Agnes, like a spoilt child.

'Give them to me NOW!' Pancake said again, her eyes blazing with anger.

Nanny Agnes meekly handed them over, 'They won't do you any good,' she sneered.

'We'll see about that,' said Pancake, and she left the cabin, locking it from the outside.

Nanny Agnes sat down and thought about what to do next.

'Hmmm. I have another little job for you, my pretty,' she said to Balthazar. 'There's no way this ship will get to Garden Island in time, but just in case, I think we'd better send Count Nasty another little message.'

She picked up her pen and began to write.

Chapter Six

My Dear Count Nasty,

The potion worked perfectly but I'm afraid there's been a little hitch in our plans. Those blasted girls found out about the potion and are going to try and make the antidote. We are now headed for Garden Island, the only place where one of the ingredients (see drawing below) can be found. YOU MUST GET THERE FIRST. Destroy all the flowers and Portia will never be a problem again. Can't wait to see you.

Yours as ever,

Agnes

Red Lima

Back in the palace of King Percy and Queen Doreen, Count Nasty stroked Balthazar's shiny black feathers. He looked closely at the drawing of the rare flower it was now his mission to destroy.

'Lord Chamberlain!' he roared.
'I need the fastest ship in the fleet
and, while you're at it, find me
a botanist.'

'A botanist, Sir?' asked the Lord Chamberlain,
puzzled.

'Yes, a botanist. That's what I said and that's what
I want!' Count Nasty snarled.

'But, Sir, I– ' begged the Lord Chamberlain.

'Don't you know what a botanist is, numbskull?'
said Count Nasty, towering over the shaking Lord
Chamberlain.

'Well... I... d... d... ' he stammered.

'Someone who knows all about PLANTS!' Count
Nasty bellowed.

'Yes, Count Nasty, right away, Sir!' said the Lord Chamberlain, shrinking away.

'And make sure he's a good one.'

'Absolutely, Sir!' and off he scurried.

On board the *Flying Pig*, Portia was rapidly driving her shipmates crazy.

'This boat is a total disgrace!' she said. 'I want it scrubbed from top to bottom and then I want it painted pink. I want the sails dyed pink, too, and I want you all to wash your clothes and hair before we get back to the palace. Boy! You, boy!' she yelled at Jim. 'How long will it be before I'm back in my lovely soft bed with my beautiful silk sheets?'

They had managed to change course to Garden Island without Portia noticing. All she was interested in was planning her wedding and doing designs for her wedding dress and bridesmaids' outfits. Poor Squawk didn't know what to do with himself and Twiggy had hardly moved from Peppermint's cabin.

'It will take another few days yet, your Highness,' lied Jim. 'We're sailing as fast as we can.'

'I demand you get me there faster,' said Portia, flouncing off. 'I'm going to look at the charts.'

'Quick, Peppermint, Pancake, stop her!' Jim whispered. 'She'll find out we've changed course.'

Peppermint and Pancake dashed over to Portia and took one arm each, turning her away from the Captain's cabin.

'Er. . . Portia,' started Pancake, trying to think of something to say. 'Nanny Agnes wants you. She's going to. . . er. . .'

Peppermint took over.

'She's going to run through the words of the marriage ceremony with you, so you'll be all ready when you get home,' Peppermint said, grinning wildly.

'Oh goody!' said Portia. She skipped off ahead of them to Nanny Agnes' cabin. Peppermint unlocked the door, waited for Portia to go inside, then quickly pulled the door shut and locked it again.

Portia span round and banged angrily on the door with her fists.

'You tricked me, you beasts! Just you wait till I get my hands on you. I'll– '

'Oh be quiet!' yelled Peppermint. Then she added quietly, 'It's for your own good. We've got to give you the antidote so that you can be yourself again.'

'I'm perfectly happy the way I am, thank you very much!' Portia whined.

'Don't worry, dear,' said Nanny Agnes. 'Count Nasty will be waiting for us at Garden Island. He's on his way there now to destroy all the flowers for the antidote before we arrive. Then we can all go back to where we belong.'

Pancake and Peppermint looked at each other in dismay and rushed off to tell Jim.

'Jim, Jim!' they shouted together. 'Count Nasty's on his way to Garden Island. He's going to destroy the flowers.'

Jim was horrified.

'All hands on deck!' he yelled. 'We need all the speed we can muster. Our futures depend on it!'

Meanwhile, Count Nasty had had considerable trouble tracking down someone who would be able to identify the flower for the antidote. The only expert he could find was a crusty, old, biology professor, who specialised in rare and endangered plants, and it had taken a lot of persuading to get him to come along. Count Nasty had to pretend they were going on a very important scientific expedition and the poor professor had been horribly seasick before they'd even left the harbour.

'Well, Professor Lupin, how are we feeling this morning?' asked Count Nasty as the grey-green-faced professor wobbled along the deck towards him.

'Oh, not so bad,' the professor said, unconvincingly. 'I'm all right as long as I. . . erm. . . excuse me. I have to. . . ' He lurched over to the side of the ship with his hand clasped over his mouth.

Count Nasty sniggered unkindly and went back to his cabin.

Chapter Seven

With only hours to spare, the *Flying Pig* reached Garden Island. Pancake packed the ingredients for the antidote into Nanny's medicine chest.

'Are you going to mix it before we get the flowers?' asked Peppermint.

'No,' replied Pancake. 'It has to be freshly made or it may not work properly. I've prepared everything else. All we have to do is put it together.'

'Ahoy, Shipmates!' called Jim from the poop deck. 'There's no time to lose. I can't see any ships but Count Nasty may well have dropped anchor on the other side of the island.' The crew looked at one another nervously. 'Is everything ready to go?'

'Aye, aye, Jim,' said Pandora. 'It's all packed in the dinghy.'

'Right,' said Peppermint. 'Let's bring Portia and Nanny Agnes on deck. I'm not leaving the old woman on board. We need her with us so we can see what she's up to.'

Pancake, Anisha and Claire went below and soon the crew heard the sound of Portia's irritating squeak.

'Get your hands off me, you'll get my dress dirty! I demand to be treated like a princess!' she squealed.

'Come on, Captain,' said Anisha. 'We're going to go on a lovely boat ride to that island over there. Doesn't it look pretty?'

'Yes!' added Bosun Betty. 'Maybe we could pick some flowers to bring back to the ship.'

'What kind of an idiot do you take me for?' Portia spat. 'I know why you want me on that island and I'm just not going!' She sat down on the deck with a thump and folded her arms.

74

'Oh yes you are!' said Peppermint, 'if it's the last thing I do. We've no time for all this nonsense. Come on, Jim. Give me a hand!' They both marched over, picked Portia up and dumped her in the dinghy. Nanny Agnes followed quietly, not wishing to suffer the same embarrassment. Portia sat at the back and sulked, as only a princess can.

'Squawk, we've got a job for you,' said Jim.

Squawk flew over to Jim, staying well away from Portia. He found it most upsetting to see his mistress like this.

'We want you to do a circuit of the island. See if you can see Count Nasty and find out what he's doing.'

'Squawk!' squawked Squawk, and flew off.

Pancake carefully placed Nanny's medicine chest in the dinghy. Safely tucked in her jacket pocket was the potion book. Everything was ready.

'If there's any trouble,' Peppermint said to Pandora, 'you and Sophie have to sail without us.'

Pandora nodded solemnly.

'Lower away,' said Jim, and the dinghy and its passengers set off for the island.

Chapter Eight

'You're all going to be in so much trouble with Mummy and Daddy when Count Nasty takes us back to the palace,' whinged Portia, pouting sulkily. 'Just you wait and see. And how long have we got to sit in this horrid dinghy? My dress is getting damp and it smells all. . . fishy. . . It's— '

'SHUT UP!!!!!' roared Jim. 'Please, Princess,' he added, blushing.

The dinghy reached the shore and they all scrambled onto the beach. Much to Nanny Agnes' amusement, Portia was driving her shipmates nuts.

'Ugh!' said the prissy princess. 'I hate sand. Once it gets in your shoes, that's it, you might as well just throw them away. And I bet that jungle is full of nasty insects and creepy crawlies and I've just manicured my nails. It's just so unfair. . .'

Pancake stuck her fingers in her ears and looked up to see Squawk flying towards them. He landed on a rock near Jim, flapping wildly.

'Nasty! Nasty! Count Nasty!' squawked Squawk.

'Oh no!' said Pancake. 'What if we're too late?'

'Judging by the way Portia's behaving, we're almost out of time anyway. She getting more annoying by the second,' said Peppermint despondently.

Nanny Agnes giggled, until she saw Pancake glare at her angrily. Portia, however, had perked up at the sound of Count Nasty's name and was trotting across the beach towards the jungle.

'I don't know about you stupid people, but I'm going to find the lovely Count,' she said, heading for the undergrowth. 'And I'll hold you *all* responsible if I break any fingernails.'

'Not so fast, Portia', said Peppermint, running
ahead of her. 'I think we'd better go first. Pancake,
have you got the chest?'

'Right here,' said Pancake, patting it fondly.

'OK, you and I will lead the way. Emily and
Anisha stay with Nanny Agnes.' They nodded eagerly.
'Jim, you and Bosun Betty bring up the rear. Let's go.'

They marched into the jungle.

Meanwhile, on the other side of the island, Count
Nasty and his party were making their way through
the thick, green jungle towards the waterfall.

Professor Lupin was so relieved to be back on dry land, he was almost skipping through the bushes, naming every plant in sight.

'Oh look, how marvellous!' he said. 'What a superb specimen of Heliconia Metallica. Quite breathtaking!' Oh my goodness!' he gasped. 'Look at those towering Alexandria palms! Do you know they bear the most fascinating flowers. They produce huge clusters of seeds which turn from green to–'

'ENOUGH!!' shouted Count Nasty, in a voice so

loud that all the birds fled from the palm trees around them. 'I mean,' he went on quietly, observing the look of surprise and alarm that had suddenly appeared on the Professor's face, 'er... let's remember what we're here for. The, er... what was it again?'

'Ah yes!' said Professor Lupin, regaining his expression of wonder. 'The rare red llima.' He paused for a moment, closed his eyes and smiled. 'Of course. Onward to the waterfall,' he continued, waving his stick. 'I believe I can hear it already.'

Count Nasty smiled his evil smile. 'Lead on, Professor Lupin,' he said.

The band of travellers from the *Flying Pig* were still some way from the waterfall, despite the fact that

Portia was striding purposefully through the jungle in pursuit of Count Nasty.

Jim shook his head sadly. 'I think we're running out of time,' he said.

Pancake saw Nanny Agnes glance at her pocket watch.

'How long have we got, Nanny?' she asked.

Nanny Agnes looked back at her defiantly.

'I'd say there's about half an hour before the effects become permanent,' she said smugly.

Emily fought back tears and Squawk shuddered. Anisha started to cry.

'Come on, everyone, don't give up!' said Pancake. 'There's still time.'

They hurried on and, only a few minutes later, emerged out of breath at the edge of a beautiful, brilliant blue lake.

'This is it!' cried Pancake. 'We've made it!'

Peppermint looked down at the ground around the lake. All she could see were trampled, shrivelled and uprooted flowers.

'Yes,' she said, 'but someone else got here first.'

She dropped to her knees in despair.

Chapter Nine

Professor Lupin and Count Nasty had reached the
lake some time before the Princess's party. And, as
they walked along the shore, Count Nasty's gang
followed close behind, trampling, uprooting and
pouring weed killer on the rare red flowers.
Professor Lupin was so excited by all the other
plants and flowers around, he didn't notice what was
going on behind him.

'So, Professor, tell me,' said Count Nasty, 'are
these the only rare red flowers of their kind on the
island?'

'Oh yes! It seems that the climate around this one lake is the only one that allows them to flourish. Most interesting, don't you think?' he said, getting out his notepad.

'Absolutely!' said Count Nasty, enthusiastically.

They were over three quarters of the way round the lake, a trail of destruction behind them, when Pancake, Peppermint, Jim and the others arrived on the other side. Immediately, Portia spotted Count Nasty near the waterfall.

'Coooeeee!' she called, 'Count Nasty, we're over h. . . *owp*!!' A hand was rapidly clamped over her mouth.

'Quiet!' said Peppermint, taking her hand away
and leading Portia and Nanny Agnes to a large rock
near the bushes. 'Sit down and shut up!' She looked
at the others tearfully. 'What are we going to do?'
she said.

'We mustn't panic,' said Pancake. 'Surely he can't
have destroyed *all* the flowers?'

'How long will it take to mix the antidote if we
do find one?' asked Jim.

'Only a few minutes,' answered Pancake, getting
down on her hands and knees to start the search.

'That means we've got about ten minutes to find a flower. Bosun Betty, you watch those two,' said Peppermint. 'Everyone else, find that flower!'

Even Squawk joined in the search. But some minutes later, when they'd had no luck, things seemed pretty desperate.

'There's nothing!' said Jim, 'Nothing at all. It's hopeless.'

'We can't give up. All we need is one little flower,'

said Peppermint, scrabbling around on the ground.

'This is all my fault! I'm so sorry! If Nanny Agnes hadn't come with me, none of this would ever have happened,' said Pancake unhappily.

'It's not your fault she's an evil old witch,' Jim said, and he kicked at a pile of stones in frustration.

Pancake watched as some pebbles splashed into the lake, then she looked back at the rest of the pile.

'EEEEEEEEEEEK!!' she screamed. 'Look!!'
There, nestling among the pile of pebbles, was one little red flower.

'Wooo hooo!' yelled Jim, dancing round in a circle. The others joined in.

'Stop!' shouted Pancake, 'There's no time for that now. We've got to make the potion. . . and quickly!'

'Bring me the medicine chest,' ordered Pancake, carefully cradling the red flower in her hand.

Peppermint brought the chest over and opened it.

'Time's running out!' said Nanny Agnes. 'Tick tock tick tock, he he he!'

'Shut up, Nanny!' said Pancake. 'Haven't you caused enough trouble?'

While Pancake concentrated on mixing the antidote, Nanny Agnes turned to Portia.

'You know, my dear,' she whispered, 'if I were you, I'd go and find Count Nasty myself.' She drew closer. 'You could sneak away while they're busy mixing the antidote. I won't tell. Then you'll be as good as home.'

Portia looked at the old woman.

'You may have something there,' she smiled. 'There's no way I'm going to take their smelly antidote anyway. But how will I get away without being seen?'

'You just leave that to me, my dear,' said Nanny Agnes in her syrupy voice. 'I'll distract them.'

She turned to Bosun Betty, who was guarding her and Portia and watching the frantic antidote making at the same time. 'Oh dear! I feel quite ill. I'm. . . I'm going to faint,' said Nanny Agnes, and she toppled sideways off the rock.

Bosun Betty ran over to help her and, as she did so, Portia darted into the bushes.

'Get the old witch some water, Anisha,' said
Peppermint, not realising Portia had escaped.
Everyone had their eyes glued on Pancake.

'OK. That's all the ingredients in the bowl. Now
hand me the pestle,' said Pancake. She ground the
ingredients into a paste. 'Now some water and a few
drops of lemon juice,' she said, mixing furiously.
'Quick, hand me the sieve, a funnel and one of those
empty bottles.

OK. Hold it still. There! It's ready! We can give it to
Portia!'

'She's gone!' exclaimed Emily.

'Oh no, she can't have! Not now,' moaned Jim.

Nanny Agnes chuckled.

Pancake strode over to where Nanny Agnes sat, just as Anisha returned with the water.

'Where is she?' asked Pancake, her eyes blazing with fury. 'Tell me now!'

'Shan't!' said Nanny Agnes.

Pancake took the water and threw it angrily at her Nanny.

'If you don't tell me I'll. . .' She took out the potion book and thumbed through it. 'I'll turn you into a dung beetle!' she said triumphantly. 'You know I can.'

Nanny Agnes considered this for a second, then pointed feebly into the bushes. 'You'll never find her anyway,' she said, turning her back on them like a sulky teenager.

Pancake, Peppermint, Jim and Emily sped off with the antidote, while Bosun Betty, Squawk and Anisha stayed with Nanny Agnes.

'If we don't catch her pretty quickly, we're done for,' said Pancake as they pushed through the jungle.

Peppermint had a brainwave.

'Hey, Emily, you're Ship's Lookout. Climb a tree and see if you can see her.'

Quick as a flash, Emily climbed the tallest tree she could find and scanned the jungle.

'There she is!' she pointed excitedly. 'She's stopped. It looks like her dress is caught on something.' Then she saw other figures in the distance.

'Uh-oh! It looks like Count Nasty's heading this way. He must've heard Portia calling.'

Pancake, Peppermint and Jim ran in the direction Emily was pointing and, sure enough, within seconds, they'd caught up with Portia. She was struggling to get her frilly dress free from the branch of a fallen tree.

'Portia!' said Peppermint, wheezing. 'Thank goodness we've found you.'

'Get away from me, all of you!' shrieked Portia. 'You just want to get me back on that smelly ship of yours!'

Pancake and Jim looked at each other. They realised that some fast talking was needed.

'Er, no, quite the opposite actually!' said Jim, trying to sound genuine.

'Count Nasty has agreed to let the rest of us stay at sea in return for bringing you back,' lied Pancake.

'Yes,' continued Peppermint. 'He's waiting for you at the lake right now with Nanny Agnes.'

The more the potion took hold, the more fluffy in the head Portia became, and she fell for their story hook, line and sinker. She jumped up immediately and carried on trying to pull her dress free.

'Oooh goody!' she twittered. 'Let's go then.'

'Just before we go,' said Pancake swiftly, 'let's have a drink to celebrate.' She took the bottle of antidote out of her pocket and held it out to Portia, smiling pleasantly. 'After all, you must be thirsty after all that running.'

'It's not very good manners to drink from a bottle,' said Portia prudishly.

'Just this once won't hurt,' Peppermint assured her. 'It's a special occasion, after all. And you can drink first so you don't catch any of our germs,' she added, trying not to sound desperate.

'Oh, all right then, just this once. I *am* very thirsty,' Portia said, taking a big gulp. 'But don't tell Da–' She stopped dead in the middle of her sentence.

Pancake and Peppermint looked at each other, then back at Portia, who stood frozen like a statue. Pancake went over and took the bottle from her hand but still Portia didn't move.

'What's going on?' asked Jim. 'Are we too late?'

'I don't know,' said Pancake, sounding worried. 'The antidote may take a while to work. We gave it to her with only seconds to spare.'

'Well, we can't just stand here. Count Nasty's on his way,' said Peppermint. She looked at Portia closely. 'Do you think she can walk?'

'There's only one way to find out,' Pancake said.
She put the bottle of antidote in her pocket and took
Portia by the arm. 'You go the other side,
Peppermint.'

They gently pulled Portia forward and, with no
change in her expression, she took a step. 'Right, it
looks as though we can get her back to the others.
Lead on, Jim.'

They unhooked Portia's frilly dress from the
fallen branch and led her carefully back to the lake.

Emily ran ahead with the news and, when Peppermint, Pancake and Jim emerged from the jungle, the others hurried over to see how Portia was.

'At least she's not complaining any more,' said Anisha, hopefully.

'Yes, but what if she stays like this forever. . .' said Bosun Betty

They all shivered.

'Let's sit her down on a rock, while we decide what to do,' said Pancake. She and Peppermint led Portia over and sat her down gently. Then they stood nearby to discuss their next move.

Chapter Eleven

'EEEEAAAAAAARRRRRGGGHHHH!!!!!'

A few minutes later, there was an ear-splitting scream. It was the most blood-curdling sound they had ever heard.

'Portia!!!' they shouted together.

'AAAAAARRGGGHHHH!!!' came the scream again. All the fish in the lake swam for cover.

Portia was standing on a boulder by the lake looking at her reflection.

'How? Why?! Who? When? What happened?!
Who has done this? Get me out of this HIDEOUS
MONSTROSITY!!' she boomed, tearing at the
frills and ribbons she'd adored only half an hour
before.

'Portia, oh Portia, thank goodness you're you
again,' cried Pancake.

Squawk flew across and landed on Portia's
shoulder, nuzzling her with his beak.

'What do you mean I'm–' Portia began. Then lots

of little flashbacks of the last forty-eight hours flooded into her head. She blushed from head to toe. Soon her embarrassment turned to blind fury. '*Where is she?*' she asked in a quiet, menacing voice that turned their blood to ice. 'Where. . . is . . . that . . . woman?'

Nanny Agnes gulped. She couldn't remember ever seeing someone look quite so angry.

Portia spotted her cowering on the other side of the clearing.

'Don't you come near me!' said Nanny Agnes. 'I'm just a feeble old woman,' she whimpered.

'Feeble, my foot!' said Portia and she stormed over.

'Don't you touch me, you bully!' Nanny Agnes wailed.

'I wouldn't touch you if you paid me,' said Portia. She looked as though she was going to explode.

Pancake and Peppermint ran over.

'What are you going to do?' they asked.

'Get my revenge, of course!'

Portia took Pancake to one side and whispered, 'If the old witch likes her potions so much, let's give her some of her own medicine. What's in the book?'

'It depends what ingredients we've got in the chest,' Pancake said, flicking through the potion book. 'We could turn her into an animal, or an insect or something?'

'Too boring. What else is there?'

'Well. . .' Pancake went on. 'There's a potion to make you older and one to make you younger, various warty type things, a love potion, one that makes your hair go green, one that makes you– '

'How does the love potion work?' Portia asked.

'The love potion?!' said Pancake, baffled. 'Well it's one that makes you fall madly in love with the first person you see. But I don't see that—'

'Excellent! My plan will kill two birds with one stone,' whispered Portia. She didn't want Nanny Agnes to hear what she was saying. 'Wait and see. You'll love it. Start making the potion, Pancake.' Portia rubbed her hands together gleefully. 'OK, let's get moving,' she continued.

'Emily, get up that tree and tell me where Count Nasty is.'

'Aye aye, Cap'n!' said Emily, delighted to be able to say 'Cap'n' again.

'Jim, bring over your penknife and cut this frill off my dress. We need a blindfold.'

'Count Nasty's coming towards us. I'd say he was about ten minutes away,' called Emily from the top of the tree. 'He's got some sort of old weirdo with a notebook with him, who's wandering off into the jungle. There are some big, beefy sailors, too.'

'We need to make sure that Count Nasty gets here first. Squawk, that's your job. When they get close, you have to flap round their faces so that Count Nasty is first out of the jungle. Peppermint, help me tear up this petticoat. We'll need it to tie Nanny Agnes to the rock.'

'Aye aye, Cap'n!' smiled Peppermint.

They tore the petticoat into strips.

'How's the potion coming along, Pancake?' Portia murmured under her breath.

'Nearly ready,' Pancake whispered back. 'Just pouring it into a bottle.'

'Fantastic!' said Portia. 'OK, shipmates, tie her up!'

Nanny Agnes was secured to the rock, moaning and complaining.

'You wait till Count Nasty catches up with you, he'll give you what for!' she whined.

'Actually,' said Portia, 'I can't wait to see him myself.'

Jim looked puzzled. But as Pancake held up the love potion, Portia continued, 'Now, Nanny Agnes, drink up!'

'I will not! What kind of an old fool do you think I am?' Nanny Agnes clamped her mouth shut.

Portia placed a blindfold over Nanny's eyes and tied it in a big bow at the back of her head. 'Oh well,' she said, 'we'll just have to make you drink it.' She stamped hard on Nanny Agnes' foot.

'Oowwwww!!' shrieked Nanny Agnes, then 'Gulp!' as Pancake poured the entire potion into her open mouth. '*Yeuch!*' she said, spitting out what she could. 'That's disgusting!'

'Quick!' said Emily, sliding down from the tree. 'He's nearly here!'

'Squawk,' said Portia, 'go and do your stuff! Everyone else, follow me.'

Portia led them into the bushes behind the rock, holding a long piece of ribbon which was attached to Nanny Agnes' blindfold.

Moments later, the tall, dark figure of Count Nasty came into the clearing. He spotted Nanny Agnes immediately.

'I see, Madam, that you've got yourself into a bit of a sticky situation,' he said with a sneer.

'Please, untie me,' said Nanny Agnes, 'Those horrid princesses have only just left. I can show you where their ship is.'

Count Nasty walked over to untie her, but as soon as he reached the rock, Portia yanked on the blindfold and it fell to the ground at his feet.

Nanny Agnes blinked her eyes and stared straight at him in wonder.

'Count Nasty, my love!' she squealed, planting an enormous smacker of a kiss on his lips as he bent down to untie her. 'My love!' she went on, 'My dear heart, light of my life, my only one...' she said, trying to wrap her arms around his neck.

Count Nasty pushed her away in dismay.

'Madam, control yourself!' he said, backing off in astonishment. 'Have you taken leave of your senses?'

There were roars of laughter from Count Nasty's gang, as they arrived in the clearing to see Nanny Agnes declaring her undying love. There was much giggling from the bushes, too.

'Count Nasty, my dearest love!' said Nanny Agnes. 'Come to me, my darling. Make me your bride!'

'You're MAD!' screamed Count Nasty, backing further and further away. Nanny Agnes lunged towards him but this was too much for the Count and he turned and fled into the jungle.

Portia and the crew rolled around on the ground in hysterical laughter.

'OK, everyone!' said Portia, wiping the tears from her eyes. 'Show's over. Let's get back to the ship!'

There was a huge cheer from the crew as the dinghy returned to the *Flying Pig*. Its passengers were all relieved to be back on board, Portia most of all. In her cabin, she took one more look at herself before changing into her Captain's clothes.

'I actually look rather good in a dress,' she said, admiring herself in the mirror, 'but it's just not me!'

She joined the rest of the crew up on deck.

They were still watching the island as the ship set sail into the sunset.

'Nanny's still chasing Count Nasty!' said Pancake, pointing to two figures running up and down the beach, followed by a big black bird. Much to Squawk's relief, Balthazar had been sent to join his mistress.

'I feel sorry for Count Nasty. . . in a way!' said Peppermint, with a snigger.

'That'll teach him to keep messing with us!' said Portia proudly. 'How long will the potion last, Pancake?'

'I've no idea,' answered Pancake, bursting into laughter. 'It should wear off in a day or so, if he's lucky!'

Portia patted her on the shoulder.

'Welcome to the crew, Pancake! And by the way,' she added with a grin, 'what's for dinner?'

West

VOYAGES

Princess
Peppermint
of
Pomerania

Princess
Pandora
of
Patagonia

Princess
Pancake
of
Pescadno